The King Has Goat Ears

To my daughters Ljudmila and Devana — KJ

Thank you to Michael and Carol for appreciating this story, Tiffany Stone for her editing job, Philippe Béha for the most inspiring illustrations, and Bojan Petrovic, my husband, for always supporting me in everything that I have done.

To Denise — PB

Published simultaneously in 2008 in Great Britain and Canada by Tradewind Books Limited www.tradewindbooks.com Distribution in Canada by Publishers Group Canada and Raincoast Books · Distribution in the USA by Orca Book Publishers · Distribution in Australia by John Reed Books · Distribution in the UK by Turnaround

Book design by Elisa Gutiérrez · Text set in Jugelia and Buttskerville

LIBRARY AND ARCHIVES CANADA CATALOGUING IN PUBLICATION
Jovanovic, Katarina, 1962-
The king has goat ears / Katarina Jovanovic ; illustrations by
Philippe Béha.
ISBN 978-1-896580-22-7
I. Béha, Philippe II. Title.
PS8619.O86K46 2008   jC813'.6   C2008-902189-4

Colour separation by Disc · Printed and bound in China. · This book has been printed on 100% ancient forest-friendly paper certified by the Forest Stewardship Council (FSC).   10 9 8 7 6 5 4 3 2

The publisher wishes to thank the Government of Canada and Canadian Heritage for their financial support through the Canada Council for the Arts, the Book Publishing Industry Development Program (BPIDP) and the Association for the Export of Canadian Books (AECB). The publisher also wishes to thank the Government of the Province of British Columbia for the financial support it has extended through the Book Publishing Tax Credit program and the British Columbia Arts Council.

The King Has Goat Ears

by Katarina Jovanovic

illustrations by Philippe Béha

VANCOUVER · LONDON

King Boyan

never left the palace.

Every time he needed a haircut,
a new barber was summoned.
That barber was never seen again.
Everyone in the kingdom
wondered what had happened
to all the barbers.

The people talked, and the king
worried.

King Boyan would not let the barbers leave the palace. He gave them different jobs. Some milked the cows, some churned butter and some took care of the pigs.

The time came for the king to have another haircut, but there were no barbers left in the kingdom.

Except for Miro.

When an emissary from the king came to his barbershop, Miro turned as white as shaving cream and fainted dead away.

"I'll cut the king's hair," said Igor, his young apprentice.

After his hair was cut, the king asked young Igor, "How do I look?"

"You look very handsome, Your Majesty."

"And what about my ears?" asked the king.

"Your ears look just fine."

"Really?" asked the king.

"Really," answered
young Igor.

So the king sent the
boy home.

Igor was scared to share with the people in the village what he knew about the king. He didn't want to tell Miro either. But he couldn't keep the secret about King Boyan to himself.

So he went to a meadow,
dug a deep hole in the
ground and shouted
down into it:

"The king has go

at ears!"

Then he covered up the hole and went home.

Igor went to the palace whenever the king needed a haircut.

The king always wanted to know about his subjects, and Igor would entertain him with stories of village life while he cut and trimmed.

"Your Majesty should come to the May Fair," Igor suggested one day. "There will be musicians, dancers, magicians, fancy cakes, everything!"

King Boyan was curious.

In the spring, long reeds grew
up out of the hole into which
Igor had shouted his secret.

Young shepherds who grazed
their flocks in the field amused
themselves by making flutes
out of the reeds.

But when the shepherds tried
to play their flutes, all they
could hear were the words:

"The king has goat ears!
The king has goat ears!
The king has goat ears!"

When the shepherds travelled into the village for the May Fair, they took the strange singing reed flutes with them to sell for a penny each.

On the day of the May Fair, the villagers were surprised to see the king's carriage driving slowly through the fairgrounds. Dark curtains hung over its windows.

As the carriage came to a
stop, a tiny voice sang out:

"The king has goat ears!
The king has goat ears!"

A guard ran over
and pulled a scared
little boy from out
of the crowd.

Just then another, louder voice came from inside the king's carriage:

"It is true. The king does have goat ears!"

And there was King Boyan, poking his face out the window and sprouting the biggest goat ears anyone had ever seen!

"Let the boy go!" he shouted to the guard.

When the king returned to the palace, young Igor was waiting for him. The boy told the story about shouting his secret into the hole, the reeds and the flute.

"Everything that happened at the May Fair was my fault, Your Majesty," he cried, throwing himself before the king. "I beg your forgiveness."

"There is nothing for me to forgive. Instead I will reward you, young barber," said the king, "for you helped me to start liking myself the way I am! Would you like jewels, gold or money?"

"I already have my reward-being Your Majesty's personal barber," answered Igor.

The barbers who had been
mysteriously locked up were
released, and almost all of
them returned home to a
big celebration.

Except for some who decided
to stay, being very much
attached to their favourite pigs.

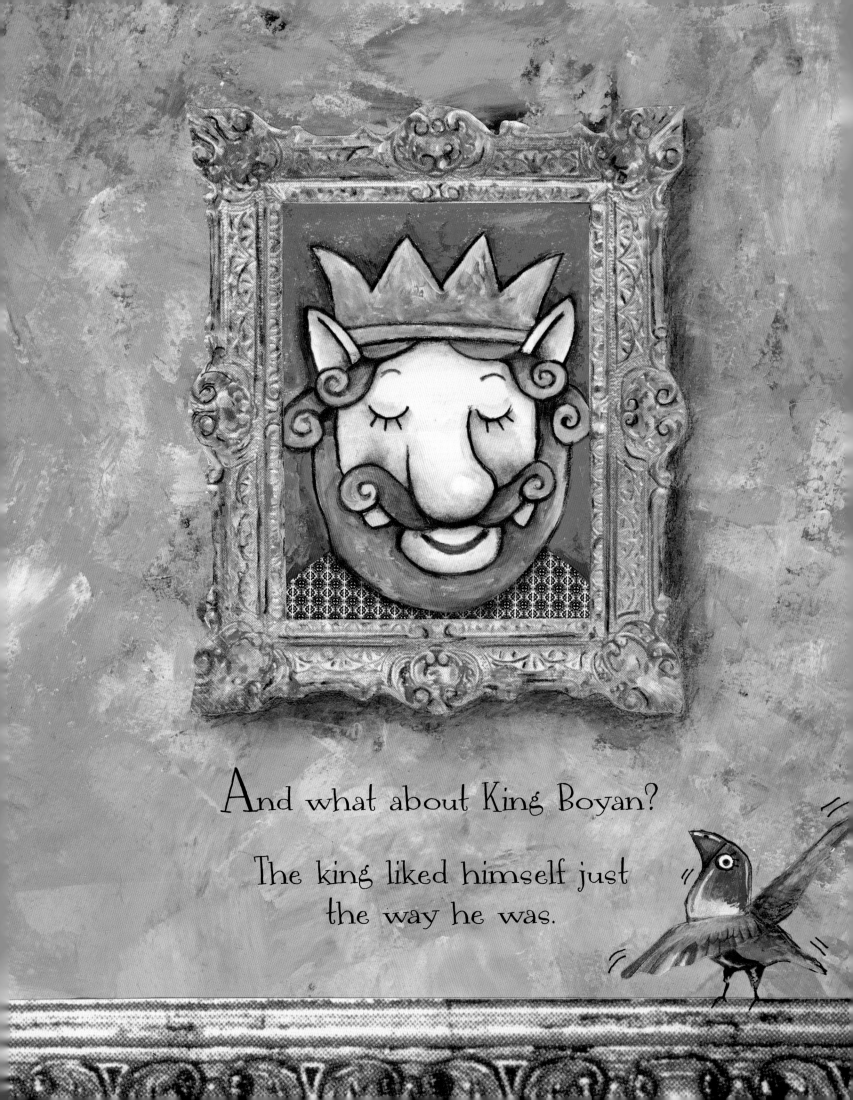

And what about King Boyan?

The king liked himself just
the way he was.